# At the

## by Kate Anderson

MW01480048

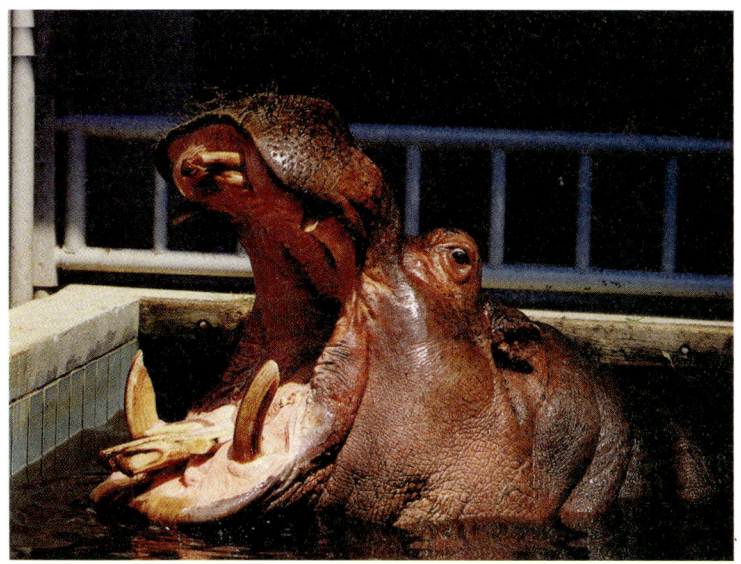

 HOUGHTON MIFFLIN     BOSTON

## Story Vocabulary

beautiful

birthday

delighted

giant

pleasant

smaller

sorry

The zoo is having a
<mark>birthday</mark>. Come see!

You can see a <mark>pleasant</mark> zookeeper.

You can see a <mark>giant</mark> hippo.

You can see ==smaller== animals, too.

You can see a <mark>beautiful</mark> peacock.

You can see beautiful butterflies.

You can be <mark>delighted</mark> by
the colors.

You will be <mark>sorry</mark> to leave.  Come back some day!